THE MAGIC HAPPY CHAIR

The Happy Magic People

Magic Best Friends -
Justine writes and dreams & Chris creates and imagines.
Lauren Greenhall brings the dreamers and the doers together.
Jameel designs and draws and makes his ideas real.
Ryan draws and colors and makes his imaginary friends real.

Thank you to the special magic bug Ally Z who is always
bursting with magic.

Meet Pearl.

She is a girl who
likes to play.

She loves to run and jump.

Sometimes she plays
with toys like these.

She is a loving sister. Sometimes she kisses the baby on the cheek as she runs by him.

Sometimes she plays with a box and she is a racecar driver…

She is also a chef and has a big kitchen.

She is a builder, a painter, a weight-lifter, a runner, and she is always Little P.

But just like you, she is very special.

She knows she is magic.

She has lots of magic inside her.

When she forgets about her magic, from time to time, she gets very sad.

When she feels sad, she does not know what to do.

The people that love her try to make her happy by telling her to go play.

"Be a racecar driver, be a chef, be a painter", they say to her.

But she doesn't want to be those things at that moment.

So she feels sad. She isn't sure who she wants to be. So she is sad.

One day when Pearl was very sad, just like this, a magic black bug with see-through wings landed on her window.

The Magic bug flapped its 'translucent' wings so fast that she couldn't stop looking at her. She saw Little P and felt her magic so she smiled at her.

Then... just as magic bugs always do, she whispered a special secret to her... "you are special magic and always happy inside."

"When you forget that, go sit in the Happy Chair. You know where it is in your house."

"Go there and remember your magic. It will always make you happy."

She wondered where this happy chair was in her house.

She looked around and around, running from room to room, searching and wondering, until suddenly .....she saw it!

How did she miss this magical happy chair that was always in her house?

Little P ran as fast as she could and jumped into the Happy Chair.

And she smiled the biggest, happiest smile that her little mouth could make.

Afterword – just remember that every time you feel confused, sad, upset or anxious you always have your chair.

It is always in your "house".

Now you go find your happy chair and make sure you sit in it every single day whenever you feel sad.

The End.

Balboa Press books may be ordered through booksellers or by contacting:

Balboa Press
A Division of Hay House
1663 Liberty Drive
Bloomington, IN 47403
www.balboapress.com
844-682-1282

Because of the dynamic nature of the Internet, any web addresses or links contained in this book may have changed since publication and may no longer be valid. The views expressed in this work are solely those of the author and do not necessarily reflect the views of the publisher, and the publisher hereby disclaims any responsibility for them.

ISBN: 978-1-9822-6514-4 (sc)
ISBN: 978-1-9822-6513-7 (e)

Print information available on the last page.

Balboa Press rev. date: 04/13/2021

BALBOA.PRESS
A DIVISION OF HAY HOUSE

From Justine – I'm grateful to
all "the people that love me" for
helping me be happy.

From Chris – Without you Sadie
Walker I wouldn't have my
happy magic chair.

CPSIA information can be obtained
at www.ICGtesting.com
Printed in the USA
LVHW070021050521
686549LV00018B/1581

9 781982 265144